Katrin Engelking

in the Valley of the Thousand Raindrops

For Ulla, Ernst, Maike and Bernd - K.E.

For Bethany, Alethea, Maia, Hannah and Ralph - R.L.

Zerwas Press
4 Stourwood Mansions
Stourwood Avenue
Bournemouth
BH6 3PP

First published in the UK in 2003

Title of the original German edition:
Anne im Tal der tausend Tropfen
© 1997 by Ravensburger Buchverlag Otto Meier GmbH,
Ravensburg (Germany)

English text © 2003 Reinhard Lindner

ISBN 0 9531830 2 5

Printed & bound by SPC Print & Design Group, UK

Anne

in the Valley of the Thousand Raindrops

Written and illustrated by Katrin Engelking

Translated by Reinhard Lindner

Zerwas Press

The beautiful princess Annabel took a deep breath
and ordered the rain
to stop immediately.

Nothing happened. It continued to rain.
Anne was angry.
How long did she have to wait for the sun to come out?
She had had enough of playing with her toys,
  she had played with them too often in the last
      few days. And playing in the garden while it
        was still raining was unthinkable. Everything
          out there was wet and unpleasant.

Anne was still thinking about the rain when she went to bed that evening.

Suddenly she heard a noise. What was it?

"Hello, Anne!" she heard somebody saying.

The voice came from the shelf. There between her toys sat a frog. Anne rubbed her eyes. A frog?

"I am Balduin", said he, hopping onto her bed and tapping indicative his head three times.

Everything in front of Anne's eyes started to become blurred like a colourful ocean. Only very slowly did things take on their usual shapes once more.

Anne couldn't believe her eyes. She was shrinking. She was now even a little bit smaller than Balduin.

Balduin grinned at her: "This way we can talk better!"
"What about?" Anne asked reluctantly. You have to be
careful with frogs which appear as if from nowhere!
"About that the rain is a wonderful thing. And not at all
boring! Where I come from, we have blissful celebrations
when it is raining", Balduin said enthusiastically.
Such a thing was impossible.
How could someone enjoy the rain?
"I would certainly not like it there!" said Anne.
But Balduin said: "See for yourself at the valley of the
thousand raindrops! Otherwise you will think I am telling
fibs!" And suddenly he hopped away.
Anne didn't have any time to be surprised that the bed cover
had changed into a meadow without her noticing. She
quickly followed Balduin, because she wanted to see the
valley of the thousand raindrops.

Balduin led Anne into a forest of unbelievably tall trees and gigantic mushrooms.

Everything was huge and strange. Anne kept looking anxiously behind her.

"This is quite normal for somebody who is as small as a frog!" Balduin calmed her down.

Anne nodded bravely, but she cautiously pressed Balduin's hand even harder.

As Anne's legs started to ache, the forest opened up. At last, they had arrived.

There was the valley of the thousand raindrops.

This wasn't an ordinary valley.
It was the finest and biggest
playground Anne had ever seen!

When Anne was quite close, she discovered many different animals, which were all very busy.

"They are preparing for the party!" said Balduin.

"It will soon start raining. And then the fun begins!"

Anne already felt the first raindrop falling onto her nose. But before she could complain, a fat rat came towards her. Anne froze.

But the rat said sympathetically: "Please, take this leaf as an umbrella. You don't seem to like getting wet."

Relieved, Anne took the leaf.

And Balduin said: "These animals are my friends. You don't need to be afraid. Come on, the party is beginning."

The rain got heavier.
All the animals assembled and a rat opened the
ceremony with a joyful shout.
The crowd cheered and drank everybody's
health with green fizzy lemonade.

Some frogs and rats played music on a stage.
They blew on blades of grass and trumpet-flowers
and the rain drummed the rhythm.
The earthworms moved graciously along with the
sound and the baby lizards and baby frogs were
happily hopping around. Some were even sitting in
puddles and were building mud-castles.
Anne gradually began to enjoy the party!
The leaf had already worn out as an umbrella. Anne
waved it through the air with the rhythm of the
music. She no longer minded that she was getting
wet.

The biggest attractions were the swings
and carousels.
The heavy rain turned the paddle
wheels faster and faster and made
everybody go round and round.
Anne screamed with joy. She wished
she could stay on the carousel forever!

Two rats hit the big gong.
The midnight soup was served!
Anne had never ever eaten such tasty soup.
Everywhere you heard only munching and the clatter
of spoons.
When the big pot of soup was completely empty,
Anne and Balduin settled down on water-lily leaves
and enjoyed the gentle swaying.
This was a jolly good party! She would never have
thought that she could have such fun when it was
raining.

Most of the animals had gone to sleep and Anne, too, would
have liked to go to bed.
Balduin guessed what she was thinking. He took her hand
and said: "You can always come back! I will take you
home!"
Anne and Balduin walked sadly home. They passed through
the wood but this time Anne didn't feel so anxious. Such
big trees were quite normal when someone was as small as
a frog.
When they arrived back at the meadow, where their journey
had started, the sun had just started to rise.

Anne was suddenly very tired.
Her eyes would simply not stay open.
She lay on the grass for just a little while.
She felt a very pleasant sensation, and she heard Balduin
whispering: "See you soon!" Then she fell asleep.

When Anne woke up, she looked around. Where had Balduin gone? And how did she get into her bed?
She stretched and yawned.
But then she suddenly had an idea.
She quickly jumped out of her bed and looked out of the window. It was still raining!
She found her raincoat and wellingtons right at the back of her wardrobe and quickly put them on.
And soon she was out in the garden, because she had a very good idea.

Anne built a huge mud-castle. A very big one, with many towers and a moat like the one she had seen in the valley of the thousand raindrops.

Sometimes she thought she'd seen a frog at the side of the sandpit, but when she looked again he was gone.

Anne was absolutely sure that one day Balduin would come back again and take her to the big rain-party in the valley of the thousand raindrops.

Also published by Zerwas Press

The little caterpillar discovers the world. She is content and likes to remain as a caterpillar. However, her siblings Cora and Conrad change – and she is suddenly alone. Then she has a wondrous encounter...

ISBN 0 9531830 1 7

Written by Judith Steinbacher

Illustrated by Antonia Nork